MARC BRO...

ARTHUR'S TV TROUBLE

RED FOX

For my friend Paula Danziger

A Red Fox Book

Published by Random House Children's Books
20 Vauxhall Bridge Road, London SW1V 2SA

A division of Random House UK Ltd
London Melbourne Sydney Auckland
Johannesburg and agencies throughout the world

5 7 9 10 8 6 4

First published in the United States of America by
Little, Brown & Company and simultaneously in Canada by
Little, Brown & Company (Canada) Ltd 1995

First published in Great Britain by Red Fox 1998

Printed in Hong Kong

RANDOM HOUSE UK Limited Reg. No. 954009

ISBN 0 09 926407 2

It all started while Arthur was watching *The Bionic Bunny Show*.

"Dogs love 'em," said the announcer. "The amazing Treat Timer. Treat your pet to a Treat Timer. Only $19.95. Treats may vary. Batteries not included. If you love your pet – get a Treat Timer!"

"Wow!" said Arthur. "Pal needs one of those."

Adverts for the Treat Timer were everywhere.

Now Arthur really wanted one.

Arthur counted his money. D.W. helped.

"Even with all my birthday money," he said, "I only have ten dollars and three cents."

"I know what you're thinking," said D.W.

She ran to protect her cash register.

Arthur decided to ask Father if he could have his pocket money early.

"Gee, I'd love to help," said Father, "but my catering business is a little slow right now."

Arthur knew Mother would understand.

"Money doesn't grow on trees," said Mother, "and I think Pal likes treats from you, not a machine."

On the way to school, Arthur was walking very slowly.
"What are you doing?" asked Buster.

"Looking for money," said Arthur. "I want to buy Pal a Treat Timer."

"Those are very expensive," said Buster. "You need a job."

"I need a miracle," said Arthur.

At school, while everyone else did a spelling test, Arthur daydreamed about the Treat Timer. Mr Ratburn asked Arthur to stay behind after school to do the test again.

Arthur took the long way home so he could think of a good excuse for why he was late. Mr Sipple was clearing out his garage.

"Hi, Arthur," he said. "Every fifty years I clean the place up. I could do with a little help."

"I could do with a little money," said Arthur.

"All these newspapers need to be recycled," said Mr Sipple.
"I'll pay you fifty cents a stack to take them out onto the
curb."

"Great!" said Arthur. "I'll do it tomorrow."

"I won't be home until after dinner," said Mr Sipple, "but
you can get started. Everything you need to do the job is
here."

"I'm rich!" thought Arthur.

All of a sudden, Arthur was in a big hurry to get home.

"I've got a job!" cried Arthur. "Now I can buy a Treat Timer!"

"Can I go to the mall with you?" asked D.W.

"Sure," said Arthur.

"I wish you were rich all the time," said D.W. "You're much nicer."

The next day, Arthur counted the stacks as he pulled them onto the curb. Twenty-four.

"That makes twelve whole dollars!" cried Arthur. "I'll come back later to collect my money!"

"You look exhausted," said D.W. when Arthur got home.
"I don't want to see another newspaper for a long, long
time," said Arthur.

"Well, then don't look out of the window," said D.W.

"So *that's* what the string was for!" said Arthur. "I'd better hurry before Mr Sipple gets home."

"Wait for me," said D.W.

"You're in big trouble," said D.W.

"You've missed some over there.

These stacks could be a lot neater.

Are you using double knots?"

"Nice work!" said Mr Sipple when he got home. "Here's your twelve dollars."

"Thank you," said Arthur.

"I helped too," said D.W. "Don't I get something?"

"You get a trip to the mall, remember?" said Arthur.

The next morning, Arthur and his family were the first
ones at the mall. Arthur put his money on the counter.
"One Treat Timer, please," he said.
"It looks bigger on TV," said Arthur when he saw the box.
"You have to assemble it, of course," said the salesperson.
"And remember, all sales are final."

Five hours later, the Treat Timer was ready.
"You're going to love it, Pal," said Arthur.
Pal sniffed it.
Arthur turned it on. It clicked. Lights flashed.

Treats shot out like rockets.

Pal let out a loud bark and ran for cover.

"Turn it off!" yelled Mother.

"I'm trying to," said Arthur. "But I think it's broken."
"And remember," said D.W., "all sales are final."
Arthur went up to his room to be alone.

"I'm worried," said Mother. "He's been up there for hours."

"I know how to get him down," said D.W.

"It's seven o'clock," she yelled up the stairs. "*The Bionic Bunny Show* is on!"

Seconds later, Arthur appeared.

"Sit down," said D.W., "so I can protect you from those nasty adverts."

"I don't need these!" said Arthur. "There's no way a TV ad will get all my hard-earned money again."

"It's the Magic Disappearing Box!" said the announcer. "Astound your friends! Eliminate your enemies! The Magic Disappearing Box from KidTricks!"

"Hmmm," said Arthur. "Now, this could be useful."

"What would you ever do with that?" asked D.W.

"Oh," said Arthur. "You might be surprised."